FIVE CLASSIC STORIES

IAN BECK'S
FAIRY TALES

OXFORD
UNIVERSITY PRESS

FIVE CLASSIC STORIES

CONTENTS

LITTLE RED RIDING HOOD

THE GINGERBREAD BOY

FIVE CLASSIC STORIES

IAN BECK'S
FAIRY TALES

OXFORD
UNIVERSITY PRESS

Great Clarendon Street, Oxford OX2 6DP

Oxford University Press is a department of the University of Oxford.
It furthers the University's objective of excellence in research, scholarship,
and education by publishing worldwide in

Oxford   New York

Auckland   Cape Town   Dar es Salaam   Hong Kong   Karachi
Kuala Lumpur   Madrid   Melbourne   Mexico City   Nairobi
New Delhi   Shanghai   Taipei   Toronto

With offices in

Argentina   Austria   Brazil   Chile   Czech Republic   France   Greece
Guatemala   Hungary   Italy   Japan   Poland   Portugal   Singapore
South Korea   Switzerland   Thailand   Turkey   Ukraine   Vietnam

Oxford is a registered trade mark of Oxford University Press
in the UK and in certain other countries

This book first published 2008
'Little Red Riding Hood', 'The Gingerbread Boy', 'The Three Little Pigs',
and 'The Enormous Turnip' first published in *The Oxford Nursery Story Book* in 1998
'The Princess and the Pea' first published in *The Oxford Nursery Treasury* in 2000

British Library Cataloguing in Publication Data

Data available

ISBN: 978-0-19-272855-5 (paperback)

1 3 5 7 9 10 8 6 4 2

Printed in Singapore

Paper used in the production of this book is a natural,
recyclable product made from wood grown in sustainable forests.
The maufacturing process conforms to the environmental
regulations of the country of origin.

THE THREE LITTLE PIGS

THE ENORMOUS TURNIP

THE PRINCESS AND THE PEA

LITTLE RED RIDING HOOD

Once upon a time lived a girl called Little Red Riding Hood. She always wore a red cape with a hood that her grandmother had made for her. She lived with her mother in a house near a deep dark forest.

One morning her mother called her.

'Granny isn't well,' she said. 'Please take this to her.' And she gave Little Red Riding Hood a basket full of good things to eat. 'Now, mind you stay on the path,' said her mother. Little Red Riding Hood promised.

After a while she saw a woodcutter.
'Hello,' he called out cheerily. 'Off to see
your granny? Well, mind how you go.'

A little later she met a cunning and hungry
wolf. He was dressed in a green coat and was
leaning against a tree.

'Good morning, little girl,' he said politely. 'What's your name?'

But all the while he was thinking what a delicious meal she would make.

'Good morning,' said the girl. 'I'm called Little Red Riding Hood.'

And she tried to walk past on the narrow path.

'Wait,' said the wolf. 'What's in that basket?'

He lifted the cloth and saw all the good things underneath.

'Delicious,' he said. 'Who are they for?'

'They are for my granny,' said Little Red Riding Hood. 'She lives just over there.'

She pointed to Granny's cottage.

'Well,' said the sly wolf, 'don't you think Granny deserves some flowers as well?'

'I suppose it can't do any harm,' said Little Red Riding Hood, and she skipped off the path, into the bluebells, and deep into the wood.

Quickly, the wolf set off down the path to Granny's cottage.

The wolf tapped lightly on the door.
'Who's there?' called Granny.

'It's me,' the wolf replied in a little voice.
'It's Little Red Riding Hood. I've brought
you a lovely basket of things to eat.'

'Let yourself in, dear,' said Granny.

So the wolf lifted the latch.

He slipped into Granny's bedroom and,
before she could cry out for help, he
swallowed her up in one big gulp.

Then he put on her night-cap and
dressing-gown, and sat in her bed.
He pulled the covers up to his chin, so that
only a tiny bit of him was
showing, and then he
waited.

Soon there came a gentle tap-tap at the door.

'Who is it?' croaked the wolf.

'It's me, Granny,' said Little Red Riding Hood. 'I've brought some flowers and a basket of good things to eat.'

'Mmmm,' said the wolf. 'Just lift the latch and let yourself in.'

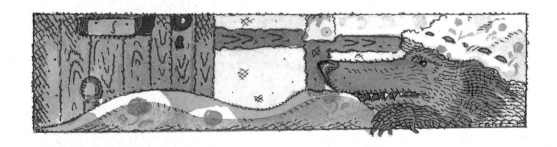

Little Red Riding Hood went into the cottage, and through to the bedroom. There she saw Granny looking much worse than she had imagined.

She went closer and sat by the bed.

'My goodness, Granny,' she said,
'what big eyes you have.'

'All the better to see you with, my dear,'
said the wolf.

'And, Granny,
 what big ears you have,'
said Little Red Riding Hood.

'All the better to hear you with, my dear,'
said the wolf.

'And, most of all,
what big teeth you have,'
said Little Red Riding Hood.

'All the better to eat you with, my dear!'
cried the wolf, and he leapt out of Granny's bed.

'Help!' screamed Little Red Riding Hood.
'You're not my granny! Help! Help!'

The wolf chased her round and round the little bedroom. He snarled and he snapped.

But at that very moment the door burst open.

There stood the woodcutter with his axe.
He struck one great blow, and the wolf
split in two.

Out tumbled Granny, safe and whole.

Little Red Riding Hood gave her granny
the basket of good things, and the big bunch
of bluebells. They all had a delicious supper,
and then the woodcutter took Little Red
Riding Hood home.

After that, Little Red Riding Hood always
stayed on the path, and never spoke to
strangers again.

The
GINGERBREAD
BOY

Once upon a time and a long time ago, there lived an old man and an old woman. They had no children of their own, so one morning the old woman decided to make them a little boy out of gingerbread.

She put two raisins for his eyes, and one for his nose, and three little candy buttons on his front.

'What a fine boy,' said her husband, and they popped him in the oven to bake.

When he was ready, they opened the oven door and out he jumped. He ran across the kitchen and out through the open door.

The old couple chased after him, calling out, 'Stop, stop, come back, you're our little gingerbread boy.'

'Stop, stop, come back, you're

our little gingerbread boy.'

But the little gingerbread boy ran on, with his cheeky smile, and he called back to them: 'Run, run, as fast as you can. You can't catch me, I'm the gingerbread man.'

'*Run, run as fast as you can.*

You can't catch me, I'm the gingerbread man.'

And the poor old man and old woman really couldn't run fast enough to catch him.

On and on ran the little gingerbread boy, out of the town and into the fields, until he met a cow.

'Moo,' said the cow. 'Stop, little gingerbread boy. I want to eat you all up.'

'Run, run as fast as you can.

But the little gingerbread boy ran on. 'I can run faster than the old man and the old woman, and I can run faster than you.

'Run, run, as fast as you can. You can't catch me, I'm the gingerbread man.'

And the cow couldn't run fast enough to catch him.

You can't catch me, I'm the gingerbread man.'

On and on, even faster, ran the little
gingerbread boy, until he met a horse.

'Neigh,' said the horse. 'Stop, little
gingerbread boy. I want to eat you all up.'
But the little gingerbread boy
ran on.

'Run, run as fast as you can.

'I can run faster than the old man and the old woman, and the cow, and I can run faster than you.

'Run, run, as fast as you can. You can't catch me, I'm the gingerbread man.'

You can't catch me, I'm the gingerbread man.'

And even the horse wasn't fast enough to catch him.

On and on, faster and faster, ran the little gingerbread boy, until he met a farmer.

'Hey, you!' called the farmer. 'Stop, little gingerbread boy. You're just what I'd like for my tea.'

'Run, run as fast as you can. You can't catch me,

But the little gingerbread boy ran on. 'I can run faster than the old man and the old woman, and the cow, and the horse, and I can run faster than you.

'Run, run, as fast as you can. You can't catch me, I'm the gingerbread man.'

And the farmer couldn't run fast enough to catch him.

I'm the gingerbread man.'

On and on ran the little gingerbread boy, until he came to a river. And there he met a clever, hungry fox.

'Why don't I help you, little gingerbread boy?' said the fox. 'Hop on my tail, and I'll swim you over to the other side.'

So the little gingerbread boy jumped on to
the fox's tail, and together they set off.

After a while, the fox said, 'You seem to
be getting wet. Why not jump further up my
back?'

So the little gingerbread boy jumped up
on to the fox's back.

When they were halfway across, the fox said, 'You're getting heavy. Why not hop up on to my nose?'

So the little gingerbread boy hopped up on to the fox's nose.

But when they reached the other side of the river the fox turned his head, snapped open his mouth, and, *crunch*, half the little gingerbread boy was gone.

'Oh dear,' said the little gingerbread boy.

Then, *crunch*, went the fox's jaws again, and the little gingerbread boy, with his cheeky grin, was all gone.

The THREE LITTLE PIGS

Once upon a time lived a mother pig, with her three little pigs. They lived happily together, but the mother pig was very poor, so she decided to send the three little pigs into the world to seek their fortunes.

They set off in the sunshine. Each carried his few treasures and some turnip tops for lunch. After a while, they reached a crossroads, and each little pig went down a different path.

The first little pig met a man carrying a large bundle of straw.

'Excuse me,' he said, 'would you give me some straw so that I may build a house?'

'Certainly,' said the man. 'It's making me sneeze ...

achoOO!'

The happy little pig built his house of straw,
and settled down to his new life.

Soon there was a knock at the door.

'Who's there?' asked the little pig.

'It's me … your friend … the wolf …
Won't you let me in?' said a growly voice.

'NO,' said the little pig. 'Not by the hair on
my chinny-chin-chin!' So the wolf said,

'Then I'll huff

and I'll puff

and I'll BLOW

your house down.'

And he huffed and he puffed, and down
fell the straw house. The poor little pig
ran off as fast as he could.

The second little pig had met a man who was carrying a bundle of sticks.

'Excuse me,' he asked, 'would you give me those sticks so I may build myself a house?'

'Of course,' replied the man. 'I've forgotten why I was carrying them in the first place.'

So the second little pig built himself a house. But soon there was a tap on the door.

'Who is it?' the little pig asked nervously.

'It's me. Your brother,' said a worried voice. 'Do let me in!'

The second little pig opened the door, and in fell his brother. He was out of breath, and just as he was about to speak, there came a loud knock at the door.

'Who's there?' asked the little pigs.

'It's me,' growled a sly voice. 'Open the door and let me in.'

'Never!' cried the two little pigs. 'Not by the hairs on our chinny-chin-chins, you shall never come in!'

So the wolf said,

'Then I'll huff

and I'll puff

and I'll BLOW

your house down.'

So he huffed and he puffed, and the house of sticks blew apart. The two little pigs ran off as fast as they could.

The third little pig had done exactly the same as his brothers. He had walked happily along the road and soon met a man who was pulling a cart laden with heavy bricks and bags of cement.

'Excuse me,' he asked, 'but might you spare me those bricks and some cement? They are just what I need to build a safe little house.'

'I'd be glad to,' said the man. 'Pulling this load is hard work.'

So the third little pig built his house. It had four square walls, and a fine chimney.

He had just settled down inside, when there came a tap at his door.

'Who's there?' he asked.

'It's us. Your brothers. *Please* let us in.'

The little pig opened his door, and in they tumbled. They were very out of breath. They had just started to speak when there came a loud knock on the door.

'Who's there?' said the little pigs.

'It's me,' said a gruff voice. 'Open the door and let me in!'

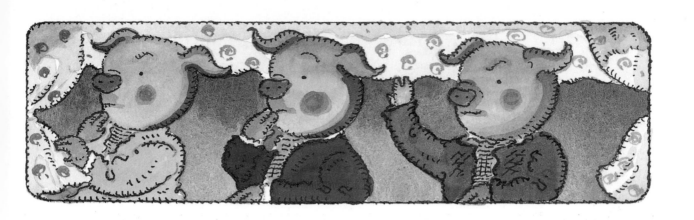

'Never!' cried the little pigs. 'Not by every hair on our chinny-chin-chins, you shall never come in.' So the wolf said,

'Then I'll huff

and I'll puff

and I'll BLOW

your house down...

and then I shall come in and eat you all up!'

The wolf drew in his breath.

He huffed, and he puffed. He puffed, and he huffed, until he could blow no more. But the little house stood firm.

The wolf was worn out. He was hungry and cross.

'I shall find another way in,' he snarled.

He began to climb on to the roof.

'He's going to come down the chimney,' said the first little pig.

'What shall we do?' said the second little pig.

'I know,' said the third little pig. 'We must build a fire.'

They set to, and soon had a good fire blazing.

The wolf lowered himself down the chimney. As his bottom inched downwards, so the flames inched upwards ... until suddenly ...

'YOWL!'

The wolf's bottom and tail were scorched and he shot out of the chimney sparking like a rocket.

The three little
pigs were never
troubled by the wolf
again. They lived happily in
the little brick house. Soon they
sent for their mother, and they
all lived happily together
for as long as they could.
Which was a very
long time.

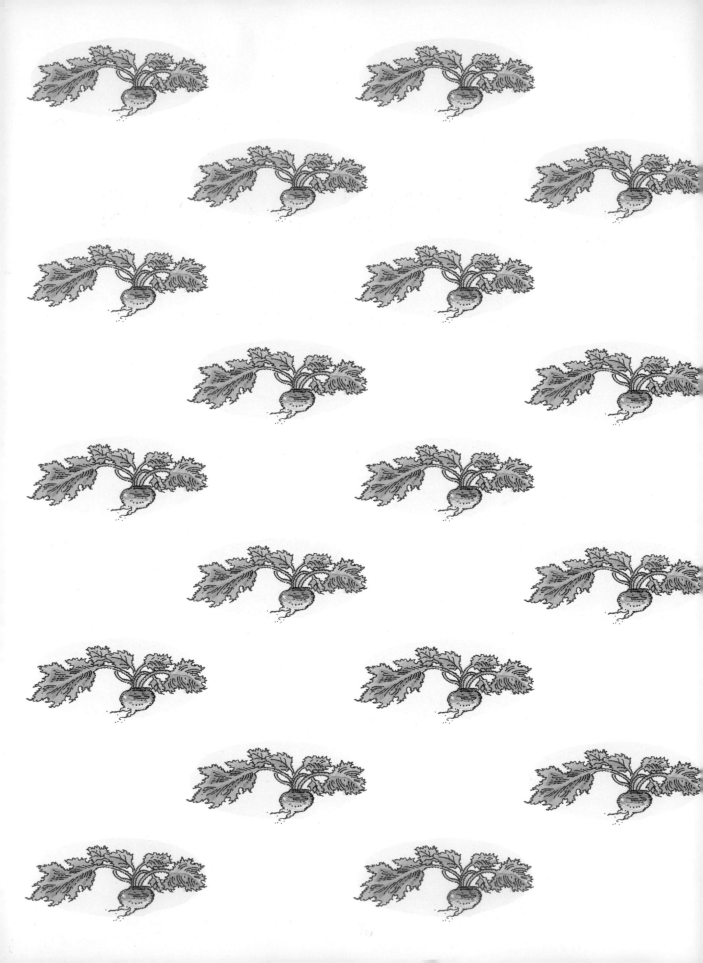

The ENORMOUS TURNIP

Once upon a time, there was a little old man. He had a fine garden, where he grew all kinds of vegetables. He looked after his vegetables and treated them very kindly. He hoed the ground, and he kept the earth free from weeds and slugs. Everyone in the village said that his were the finest vegetables, best for colour and best for flavour.

Now, the little old man had a secret. When all his seeds were planted and the little seedlings were just popping their heads out of the ground, he would talk to them. And this is what he would say: 'Come on, you little seedlings, grow, grow!' He said it over and over, every evening before he went to bed.

Come on, you little seedlings, grow, grow!

His wife would shake her head and say that he was a fool – no good could come of talking to vegetables. She said that it was her careful watering that gave them such a fine crop.

One day the little old man planted out some turnips. His wife watered them well, and in time up popped the seedlings. 'Come on, you little seedlings, grow, grow!' said the old man, and grow they did.

One of them grew much bigger than the rest. It kept on growing, and growing, until it took up a whole corner of the garden.

Every morning the old man would come
out and look at his turnip. He would give
it a little pat, and talk kindly to it. The
turnip kept on growing, until it took up
half the garden.

One morning his wife said, 'It's time to pull up that great turnip – there's enough there to feed the whole village.'

So the old man went out and began to pull up the enormous turnip. He pulled and pulled, but it wouldn't move. The old man called out to his wife, and his wife came and she pulled at the old man, and the old man pulled at the turnip, but it wouldn't move.

So the wife fetched a boy who lived nearby, and the boy pulled at the wife, and the wife pulled at the old man, and the old man pulled at the turnip, but still it would not move.

So the boy went to fetch his little sister, and the little sister pulled at the boy, and the boy pulled at the wife, and the wife pulled at the old man, and the old man pulled at the turnip, but still it would not move.

So the little sister ran to fetch her dog, and the dog pulled at the little sister, and the little sister pulled at the boy, and the boy pulled at the wife, and the wife pulled

at the old man, and the old man pulled at the turnip, but still it would not move.

So then the dog was sent to fetch his friend the cat, and then the cat pulled at the dog, and the dog pulled at the little sister, and the little sister pulled at the boy, and the boy pulled at the wife, and the wife pulled at the old man, and the old man pulled at the turnip, but still it would not move.

So then the cat was
sent to fetch her friend
the little mouse, and
then the mouse pulled
at the cat,

and the cat pulled
at the dog,

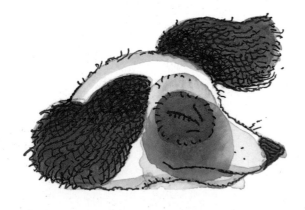

and the dog pulled
at the little sister,

and the little
sister pulled
at the boy,

and the boy
pulled at the wife,

and the wife pulled
at the old man,
and the old
man pulled
at the
turnip.

Whoosh! The turnip burst out of the ground and the old man fell on the wife, the wife fell

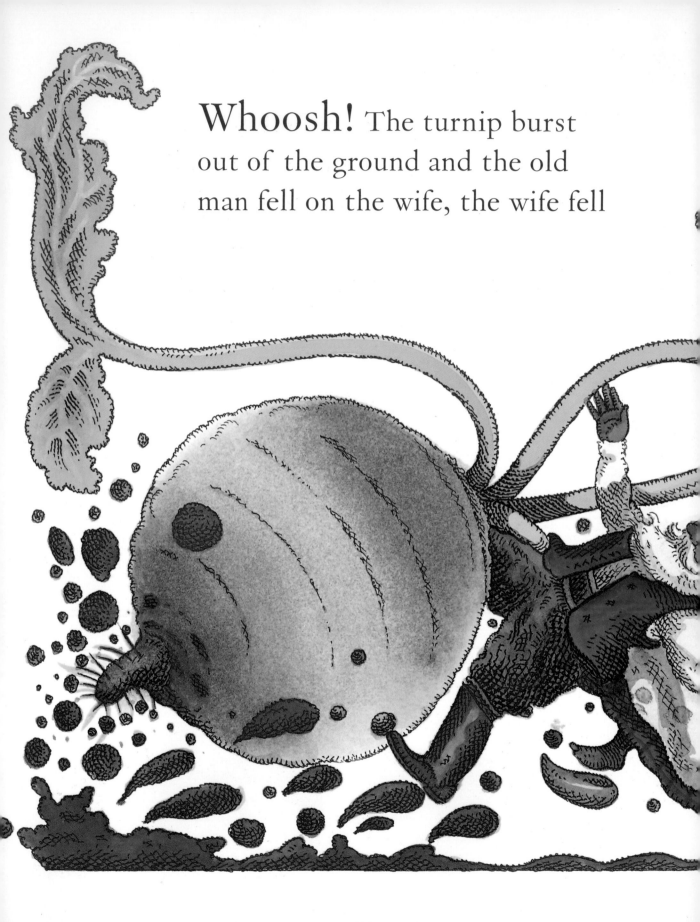

on the boy, the boy fell on the
little sister, the little sister fell
on the dog, the dog fell on the
cat, and the cat fell on the
little mouse, who said, 'Eeek!'

Eeek!

After they all brushed themselves down, they set to and made a great feast with the enormous turnip, and the whole village joined in and made a party of it.

The PRINCESS
and the PEA

Once upon a time, in a faraway kingdom, there lived a prince. For his twentieth birthday he was given a fine white stallion, called Blaze.

Soon afterwards the king sent for him.

'My boy,' he said, 'it is time you set out and found yourself a real princess to marry.'

So the prince travelled the length and breadth of the world on Blaze. They rode in the summer sun and winter snow, through deserts and over mountains.

The prince met many girls who said that they were princesses. Girls who curtsied very nicely. Girls with eyes hidden behind painted fans. Girls who danced elegantly in bright, silk dresses.

But after all his travels he had never been sure whether any of the girls he had met had been a real princess.

And so, one night, the prince rode back into the palace yard, with his head bowed and a heavy heart. His mother welcomed him back with his favourite meal.

'Come on,' she said. 'Sausages, onion gravy, and mashed potatoes. That ought to cheer you up.'

But even after a hearty supper the prince was still sad. 'I've looked over the whole world, from one end to the other. I'll never find a real princess,' he sighed.

'Don't worry,' said the queen, 'there are ways of telling a real princess. When the right girl comes, I will find out for you, never fear.'

Summer turned to autumn, and great storms shook the kingdom. Hailstones the size of goose eggs crashed around the palace turrets. A great wind tore up the mighty oak tree that the prince had loved since he was a boy.

Winter came, howling in on a blizzard, and the palace was surrounded with deep drifts of snow; even Blaze was kept in the stable under fleecy blankets.

Then one night, the coldest of the year so far, when even the powdered snow had frozen into hard ice, there was a knocking at the palace door. The king was roused from his warm fireside. 'Who on earth can that be out in this awful weather, and at this late hour?' He set off, wrapped in his warmest cloak, and opened the heavy door.

A girl stood knee-deep in a drift of snow. Her fine cape, reduced to rags, was wrapped around her shoulders, and she was huddled and shivering. Her hair was wet around her face, and there were little icicles on her sooty eyelashes.

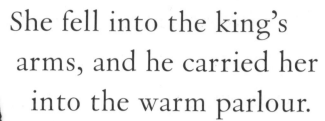

She fell into the king's arms, and he carried her into the warm parlour. After a few minutes the girl was warmed through. She sat by the fire, drinking a cup of hot chocolate. Some colour had come back into her cheeks, and as she brushed the damp strands of hair away from her face, the prince could see that she might just be beautiful.

The queen glanced at her son and saw that he was gazing at the mysterious girl. 'Tell us about yourself, my dear,' she said.

'I am Princess Phoebe,' said the girl. 'I have been travelling the world, seeking a suitable prince to marry.' She shook her head sadly. 'I have searched for nearly a year with no luck, for you see he must be a real prince. I was just on my way home when the blizzard struck. I stabled my poor horse, and then followed the lights here.'

The prince was about to speak out when the queen gestured to him to be quiet.

'You must be exhausted, my dear,' she said brightly. 'Go and have a hot bath and a good sleep, and in the morning all shall be well.'

While Phoebe was in her bath, the queen took the prince and two servants to the guest bedchamber. She ordered the servants to strip all the bedding from the bed and take off the mattress. Then the queen took a little silver box from her purse. Inside was a single green pea.

The queen took the pea and placed it on the bed base. Then she ordered the servants

to bring as many mattresses and feather quilts as they could find, and place them all on top of one another. The pile reached almost to the ceiling, and it was a very tall room.

'Now we shall see if she is a real princess,' said the queen. 'Trust me.'

Princess Phoebe spent an uncomfortable night. Despite mattresses, feather quilts, and cosy warmth, things weren't right. No matter how she lay in the bed, no matter how she twisted and turned, she couldn't settle and she didn't sleep a wink.

In the morning, all looked beautiful in the bright sunshine. This would be a fine place to live, Phoebe thought. She went down to the parlour for breakfast.

'Good morning, my dear,' said the queen. 'I hope you slept well.'

Phoebe's eyes had dark circles round them. 'I couldn't sleep at all,' she said. 'No matter how I lay in the bed something was digging into me. I must be covered in bruises.'

It was then that the prince understood. If this girl had felt such a tiny thing as a pea through all those layers of quilts and feathers, then she must be a real princess.

'Look around you, my dear,' said the queen. 'You will see that this is no ordinary house – it is a palace.'

Phoebe looked at all the silverware on the breakfast table, and at the fine silks at the tall windows. At that moment the king entered, with his lord chamberlain.

'If this is a palace,' said Phoebe, 'then you must be the queen, and there, if I am not mistaken, is the king.' At that she curtsied, and then bounced up with a smile on her face. 'Which means that your son is a real prince.'

Later that day the princess's horse was
brought from the stables, a fine black mare
with a long silky tail. Together the prince
and princess set off to ride in the bright
winter sunshine.

'Mark my words,' said the queen, 'we'd
best set the lord chamberlain to preparing
the cathedral for a royal wedding.'

And so they did, and later that year the real prince and the real princess were married, and went to live in their own palace by a lake.

Soon they had to add a nursery, and they all lived happily to the end of their days, which was as long a time as it could be.